Copyright © 2009 by MacKenzie Smiles, LLC

MacKenzie Smiles, LLC
San Francisco, CA

www.mackenziesmiles.com

Originally published as *Når to sier godnatt*
Copyright © Gyldendal Norsk Forlag AS 2002 [All rights reserved]
www.gyldendal.no

Original text by Tor Åge Bringsvaerd
Original illustrations by Tina Soli

Translated by Tonje Vetleseter

Art production by Bernard Prinz

ISBN 9780981576138

Printed in China

10 9 8 7 6 5 4 3 2 1

Distributed in the U.S. and Canada by:
Ingram Publisher Services
One Ingram Blvd.
P.O. Box 3006
LaVergne, TN 37086
(888) 800-5978

Tor Age Bringsvaerd

when two say goodnight

Illustrated by Tina Soli

Translated by Tonje Vetleseter

MACKENZIE
SMILES
San Francisco

When **two cats** say goodnight...

...they lick each other's ears.

when two **pigs** say goodnight...

...they **curl up** their **tails** and look **deep**

into each other's **eyes**.

When two **giraffes** say goodnight...

...they wrap **their** **necks** around **each** other and whisper **secrets.**

when two **clowns**

say **goodnight...**

...they laugh so **hard** they almost wet their **pants.**

when **two** kings say goodnight...

...they take off **their** crowns and pat each **other** on the **head**.

When two
ghosts
say goodnight...

...they blow cold air on each other until their teeth chatter.

When two **dinosaurs** say goodnight...

...they **roar** so **ferociously** that **even** the cows are afraid.

when **two** cheese **sandwiches** say goodnight...

...they snuggle up **next** to **each** other

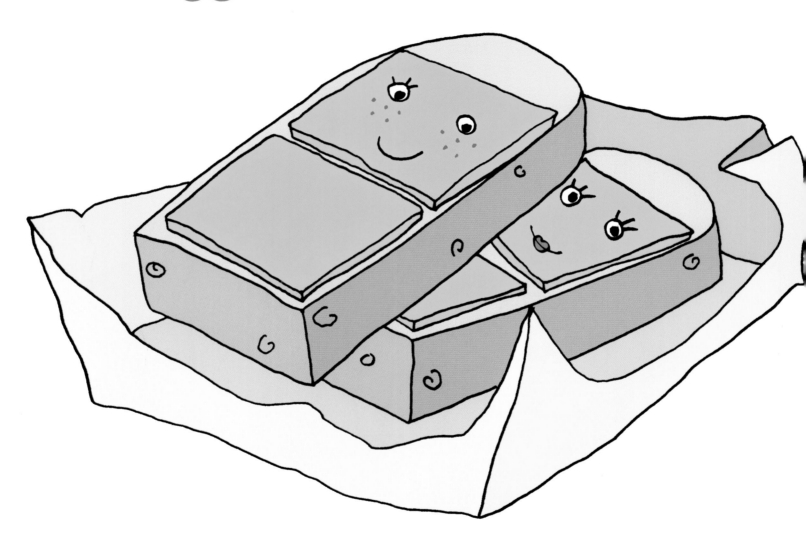

and **play** packed **lunch.**

when two **washcloths**

say goodnight...

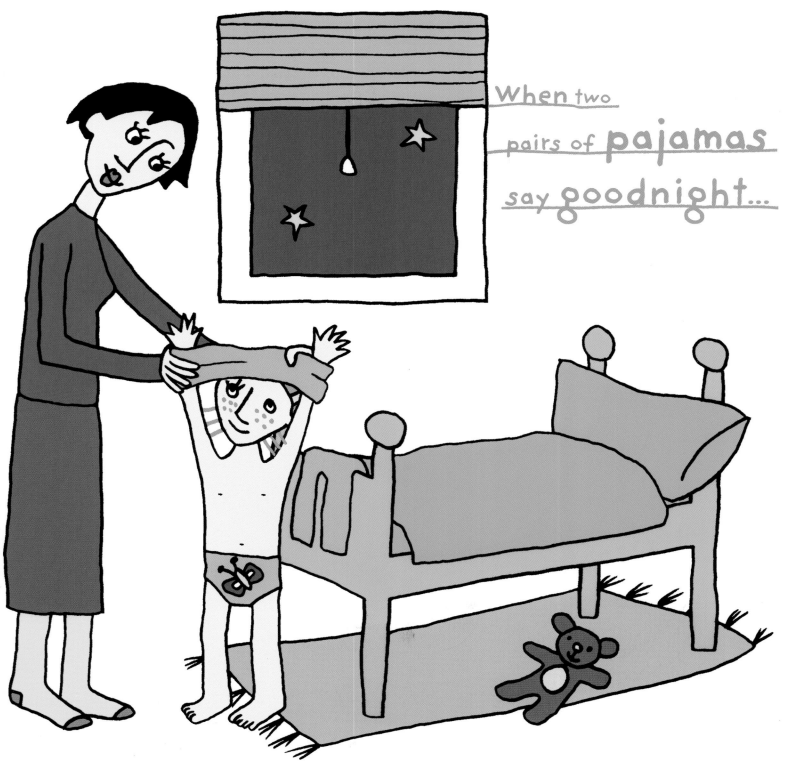

When two pairs of **pajamas** say **goodnight**...

When Mommy and **I** say goodnight...